1 stuffed toy &
1 BOOK

MANATEE WINTER

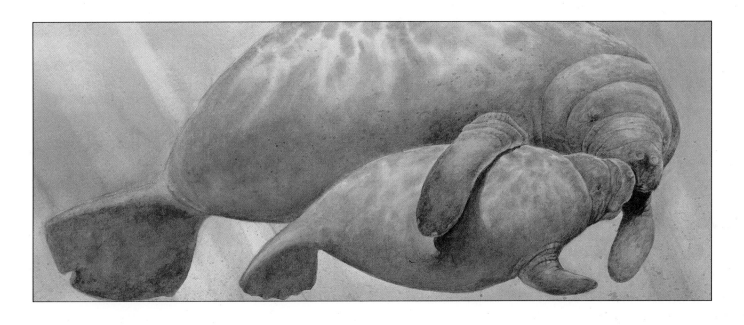

by Kathleen Weidner Zoehfeld   Illustrated by Steven James Petruccio

Soundprints
Where Children Discover...

For Geoffrey
—K.Z.

For Marie and Albert Petruccio,
my mom and dad, with my love for theirs
—S.P.

Book copyright © 1994 Trudy Corporation, 353 Main Avenue, Norwalk, CT 06851,
and the Smithsonian Institution, Washington, DC 20560.

Soundprints is a division of Trudy Corporation, Norwalk, Connecticut.

Book Design: Shields & Partners, Westport, CT

10 9 8 7 6 5
Printed in Singapore

Acknowledgements:
   Our very special thanks to Dr. Charles Handley of the department of vertebrate zoology at the
Smithsonian's National Museum of Natural History for his curatorial review.

Library of Congress Cataloging-in-Publication Data

Zoehfeld, Kathleen Weidner.

Manatee winter / by Kathleen Weidner Zoehfeld ; illustrated by Steven James Petruccio.
         p.   cm.
Summary: A mother manatee and her little calf travel from the Gulf of Mexico through
dangerous water full of speeding boats.
         ISBN 1-56899-075-8
1. Manatees — Juvenile fiction. [1. Manatees — Fiction.]
I. Petruccio, Steven, ill. II. Title.
         PZ10.3.Z695Man 1994   94-158
         [E] — dc20   CIP
                                                                    AC

HAJBC

Prologue

There are only about 1800 West Indian manatees left in North America, and they are listed as an endangered species. Living mainly around the coast of Florida in estuaries and bays and in Florida rivers, these curious and gentle creatures have no natural enemies. Once hunted for their meat and hides, today manatees are protected by law from human hunters and poachers. However, many manatees are killed accidentally every year in collisions with speeding boats, in spite of boating regulations in some areas where manatees gather. Also, as new houses and businesses are built along the coastline and near the riverbanks, the seagrasses the manatees feed on are often destroyed.

As more and more people come to live and play along the Florida coast, manatee lives are threatened. Now only the care and concern of people can save the manatee from extinction.

This book is about one West Indian manatee and her little calf.

A cold November wind blows, chilling the north-west coast of Florida and stirring up the waters of the Gulf of Mexico.

Underwater, a huge gray manatee paddles lazily. Her six-month-old calf swims by her side.

Below them, a tuft of seagrass sways invitingly, and Mother manatee stops to browse. Little Calf nibbles and waits.

Mother rises to the surface, and Little Calf follows. They reach their noses up above the choppy waves to take a breath.

Mother is alarmed by the cold air on her nose. Soon the water will be getting colder, too. She must get her calf to warmer waters. No manatee can endure the winter chill of the Gulf. For a calf, the cold is especially dangerous.

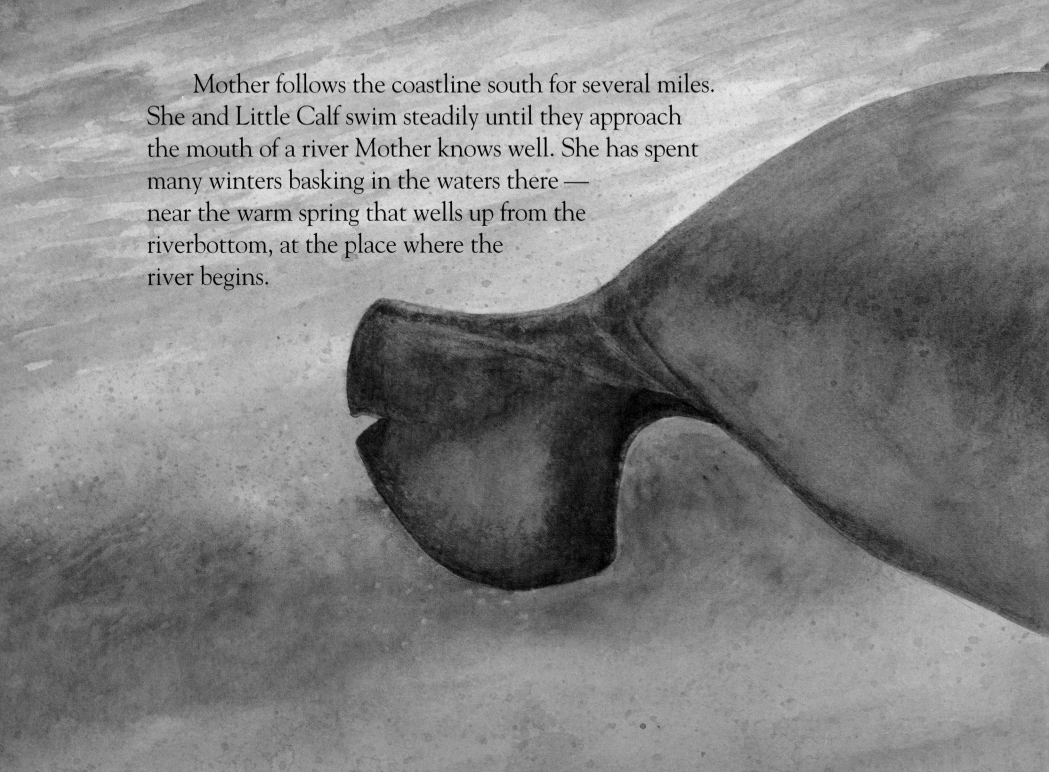

Mother follows the coastline south for several miles.
She and Little Calf swim steadily until they approach
the mouth of a river Mother knows well. She has spent
many winters basking in the waters there —
near the warm spring that wells up from the
riverbottom, at the place where the
river begins.

8

As they turn up the river, Little Calf nuzzles Mother and squeaks with hunger. She relaxes and lets him nurse and rest. The safety of warm spring water is not far away now.

Then, as Mother dozes, Little Calf wanders off. He begins to nibble at some water-weeds near the riverbank.

Suddenly — BROOOOM! — he hears a sharp roar overhead. A dark shadow darts past. He screams in fear.

Mother squeals for him to come to her side — down on the riverbottom.

Just a little way up the river, the dark form slows and then stops. It is a boat, dropping anchor. All is quiet.

Slowly and carefully, they swim over to investigate — nuzzling and rubbing the boat with their muzzles.

Tap, tap, tap — thump, thump — the boat makes a strange noise. Startled, Mother stops their exploration. She leads Little Calf away, as fast as their big tails can take them. Besides, now even the river-water feels chilly. Mother must get her calf to the warm spring.

But the river is busy with boats, zooming here and there. She leads Little Calf through the maze of activity.

17

BROOOOOM! A boat comes up behind them. Mother screams to Little Calf, and they dive, thrashing their tails and churning the water into foam.

Mother reaches the bottom, safe from the cutting blades of the boat's propellers. Mud clouds the water around her. She peers through the murk.

Little Calf has disappeared!

She squeaks for him frantically. But the roar of the motorboat drowns out her call.

Lost and confused, Little Calf looks for a place to hide. He spots a dense clump of water-weeds and plunges in, head first.

But he cannot hide in the weeds for long. He must get to the surface for a breath of air. As he works his way up through the weeds, thick stems wind around his flippers and hold him fast.

Squeak, squeak! He calls for his mother.

Mother hears his squeak in the distance and follows his call.

She can barely see him, struggling in the knot of weeds. She swims closer and nudges him. Encouraged, he wiggles harder, pulling himself through the tangle of stems.

She guides him to the surface for a breath. They press on upriver, Little Calf clinging close by Mother's side.

When they finally arrive at the spring, the sun is setting, and the air is growing colder. Mother lets herself sink down to the warm, sandy bottom. Little Calf settles comfortably on her tail. They close their tiny eyes and snooze for a while, basking in the spring's warmth.

Every few minutes, they bob up to the surface to breathe. They are tired from their long swim, and the air feels so cold that they huddle near the warm spring all night.

26

Early next morning, bright rays of sunshine shimmer through the clear blue-green waters. One by one, other manatees have come from far and wide to warm themselves in the waters of the spring.

Little Calf follows Mother through the small crowd, as she walks with her flippers along the bottom.

Soon he notices some other calves who have just arrived. Living alone with his mother all summer in the vast Gulf-coast waters, he has never seen another young manatee before.

He bumps a year-old calf with his nose, curious to see what the little manatee will do. They nibble each others' backs in a friendly way. Then they tumble and play.

While Little Calf glides upside down near the bottom, an old bull wakes up and stretches. His big tail swings up and thumps Little Calf by accident.

Little Calf squeals in surprise. Mother swims over and gently nudges Little Calf away from the sleepy bull.

Little Calf and his mother kiss and hug. Together they cruise away, exploring every corner of their winter home, always looking for more good plants to eat.

Throughout the cold winter, Mother and Little Calf will remain near the spring. On sunny days, they may venture downriver in search of seagrasses. But they never stay away long from the warmth and safety of the spring.

About the Manatee

Manatees are mammals that spend all their lives in water. They are quite unusual in that they thrive in both fresh and salt water. Like all mammals, manatees are warm-blooded and breathe air. They are among the world's larger mammals, some growing to be as big as 13 feet long and weighing about 1300 pounds. Individual manatees may live as long as 30 years.

In the warm summer months, some manatees travel as far north as Virginia or as far west as Louisiana, but, wherever they go, the water they swim in must be warm for them to survive. As winter comes, the manatees return south and swim up many of Florida's shallow rivers and waterways in search of warmer waters, where they congregate in small groups.

For more information about manatees or manatee adoptions, please contact the Save the Manatee Club, 500 North Maitland Avenue, Maitland, Florida, 32751, or call 1-800-432-5646.

Glossary

bull: An adult male manatee.

coastline: The boundary line that is formed where the land meets the sea.

gulf: A large area of ocean surrounded on three sides by land.

river: A large natural stream of fresh water.

seagrass: Any of a variety of grasses, such as turtle grass, manatee grass and star grass, that grow underwater.

spring: A source of water coming from underground. Spring water can be warmed by the natural heat deep within the earth's crust.

water-weeds: Any of a variety of aquatic plants.

Points of Interest in this Book

pp. 4-5, 18-19, 20-21, 24-25 seagrass.

pp. 6-7, 10-11, 20-21, 24-25 striped mullet.

pp. 12-13, 20-21 red mangrove roots.

pp. 20-21 bay scallops.

pp. 22-23 egret, red mangrove trees.